D0030385
YO-KAI WATCH™
1
STORY AND ART BY
NORIYUKI KONISHI
ORIGINAL STORY AND SUPERVISION BY LEVEL-5 INC.

YO-KAI WATCH

Volume 1

NATE'S LUCKY DAY

Perfect Square Edition

Story and Art by Noriyuki Konishi

Original Story and Supervision by LE

Translation/Tetsuichiro Miyaki
English Adaptation/Aubrey Sitterson
Lettering/William F. Schuch
Design/Izumi Evers
Editor/Joel Enos

Published by VIZ Media, LLC
P.O. Box 77010
San Francisco, CA 94107

10 9 8 7 6 5 4 3 2 1
First printing, November 2015

STORY AND ART BY
NORIYUKI KONISHI

ORIGINAL STORY AND SUPERVISION BY LEVEL-5 INC.

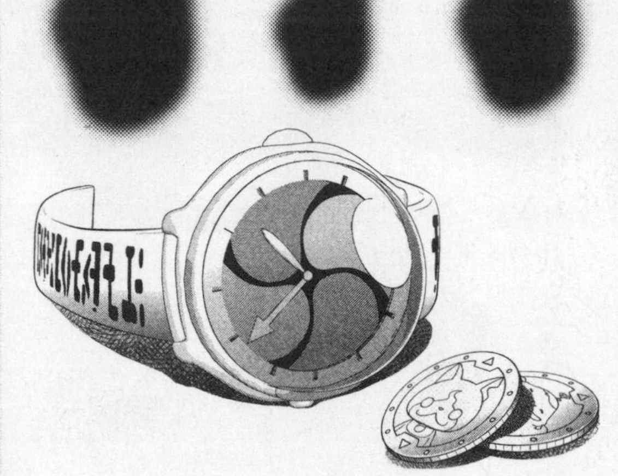

Table of Contents

CHAPTER 1: MY FIRST YO-KAI FRIEND!

FEATURING JIBANYAN

I'M NATE ADAMS.
JUST AN ORDINARY ELEMENTARY SCHOOL STUDENT.
I'M NOT SUPER SMART. I DON'T RUN FAST.
I'M ORDINARY!
BASEBALL, SOCCER, VIDEO GAMES...
THERE'S NOTHING SPECIAL OR UNIQUE ABOUT ME AT ALL. I'M SIMPLY...
...AN ORDINARY ELEMENTARY SCHOOL STUDENT!
BUT ONE DAY...

...I CAME ACROSS SOME-THING STRANGE ...
HUNH... I DON'T REMEMBER THIS TREE BEING HERE...
WHAAAAM!
A CAPSULE MACHINE?!

KACH-CHUNK
DOES IT WORK?
LOOKS LIKE I GOT A DUD.
THOOOM!
WHOA!
TUUNGK!
A ROCK ?!

WOOOSH
?!
HOW DARE YOU CALL ME A DUD!
...!
VRRRRM

THOOOM!
I'M WHISPER, THE YO-KAI BUTLER! ♪
AT YOUR SERVICE!
TO THANK YOU FOR RELEASING ME, I WILL BECOME YOUR PERSONAL BUTLER!
WHISS ♪ ♪
WHAT?
YO...
YO...

YO-KAI?!
I'M SORRY TO STARTLE YOU. HUMANS CAN'T NORMALLY SEE US! ♪
VOOSH
VOOSH
VOOSH
YOU WANT TO KNOW WHY YOU CAN SEE ME? WELL, THAT'S BECAUSE ...
YEAH ...?
WAIT!
DON'T YOU WANT TO HEAR WHAT I WAS DOING INSIDE THAT STONE BALL?!
VUFF
VUFF
DON'T CHA? DON'T CHA?
HUNH HUNH
UH... UM...
GASP!
OH NO! WHAT KIND OF BUTLER AM I?! I HAVEN'T EVEN ASKED IF YOU NEED ANYTHING!
IS THERE ANYTHING I CAN DO FOR YOU?
...
A WISH, MAYBE?
SOMETHING I CAN GET YOU? SOMETHING I CAN HELP YOU WITH?
VOOSH VOOSH
VOOSH VOOSH
OH, UH... UMM ...
NOTHING?! IF YOU DON'T HAVE ANYTHING RIGHT NOW, FEEL FREE TO TELL ME WHEN YOU DO. ♪
IN THE MEANTIME, ALLOW ME TO TELL YOU MORE ABOUT MYSELF!
VOOSH
VOOSH
VOOSH
...!

THIS IS SO MUCH EASIER TO DO WHEN THE HUMAN DOESN'T RUN AWAY FROM ME!
YOU HAVEN'T EVEN BEEN BOM-BARDING ME WITH QUES-TIONS!
I'M JUST... TOO SHOCKED TO ASK YOU ANYTHING!
TING
YOU KNOW, I...
VOOOSH
...REALLY LIKE YOU! YOU SEEM LIKE A NICE, ORDINARY GUY!
AND YOU SEEM LIKE A PAIN IN THE NECK!
IS THIS A REAL YO-KAI...? HE'S NOT EVEN TRYING TO EAT ME OR ANY-THING!
YOU MIGHT BE ABLE TO BRIDGE THE GAP BETWEEN THE HUMANS AND THE YO-KAI.
VOOOSH
VOOOSH
YES, YES, I THINK YOU CAN!
WAIT, WHAT? BRIDGE THE GAP?!
SCHIIIING
!
ALLOW ME TO GIVE YOU A GIFT!
FWEEEEEEE

?!
THE YO-KAI WATCH!
PRESS THE BUTTON ON THE RIGHT! ♪
HURRY UP, HURRY UP!
SEEING IS BELIEVING! FEAR IS WORSE THAN ANY DANGER!
VOOSH
VOOSH
MAKE HASTE!
OH, UH... OKAY ...
VOOSH
UHM ...
THE BUTTON.

THOOOOOM
WHOA!
FWOOOOOSH
PRETTY COOL, RIGHT?
BUT THAT'S OKAY. HAPPY, HAPPY!
UHH...
AND YOUR WATCH'S LIGHT WILL HELP YOU SEE US!
FWOOOSH
NOT OVER HERE. ♪ AND NOT OVER THERE. ♪ LOST! LOST! ♪
WE YO-KAI ARE EVERY-WHERE!
WHERE DID YOU COME FROM ?!

WHEEEEEE
NOOOPE. ♪ BUT LIFE IS STILL WONDERFUL! ♪
WHY AM I ACTING LIKE THIS?!
HA HA HA... YOU'RE FEELING THE EFFECTS OF A YO-KAI!

THE YO-KAI YOU JUST SAW IS HAPPIERRE.
HE MAKES EVERYONE AROUND HIM HAPPY!
OOOOH, REALLY? ♪
MANY UNEXPLAINABLE THINGS IN THIS WORLD ARE ACTUALLY THE WORK OF YO-KAI!
VOOSH VOOSH VOOSH VOOSH
OOOH. ♪
BUT PEOPLE USUALLY JUST WRITE THEM ALL OFF AS COINCI-DENCE OR THEIR IMAGINA-TION...
HMMM. ♪
SHIIING SHIIING
ARE YOU EVEN LISTENING TO ME?

NOPE, NOT AT ALL. ♪
OOOH, A KITTY-CAT!
HUUUNH?!!
NOT AT ALL?!
FWAAASH...
VNNNN
FWAAASH
I CAN'T SEE IT UNLESS I'M SHINING THE LIGHT RIGHT ON IT.
VNN
VOOOSH
HUNH?!
VRROOM
LOOK OUT!
TIIIING
SHUNK!

CHOOM
CHOOM
TAKE THIS, CAR!
PAWS OF FURY!
CHOOM
CHOOM
I THINK HE'S TRYING TO FIGHT THE CAR!
HUNH? BUT WHY ?!
MEOW MEOW MEOW MEOW MEOW MEOW!!
CHOOM

MRRAAAOW!
THUNCK
THE CAR RAN RIGHT INTO HIM!
HUMANS CAN'T SEE US, AFTER ALL...
THOOOM
I'M SO... LAME!
THOOM
I... I...
I... LOST AGAIN...
NNNNNGH
OH! DO YOU... DO YOU KNOW AMY?!
?
!
A HUMAN?! YOU CAN SEE ME?!
ARE YOU OKAY ?!

VSH VSH
NO, NO, NO!
I HAVE TO KEEP IT TO-GETHER!
IF YOU'RE IN NEED OF HELP, MY MASTER WILL BE MORE THAN HAPPY TO LEND YOU A HAND.
VOO—OSH
HEY!
?
I USED TO BELONG TO A GIRL NAMED AMY.
BUT I WAS RUN OVER BY A CAR AND KILLED... AND WHEN AMY SAW ME...
YOU'RE SO LAME...
HUNH?! HOW COULD SHE?!
NO WAY!
PURE EVIL...
NO ...

AAARGH!!
AMYYYYYY!!
IT'S MY FAULT. I SHOULDN'T HAVE DIED IN A MEASLY LITTLE CAR ACCIDENT!
SO I WANT TO BECOME A MIGHTY CAT THAT CAN DEFEAT CARS...
... SO I CAN RE-TURN TO AMY!
NO! IT'S NOT YOUR FAULT!
THUNGKT
CAAAAAAAR! PAWS OF FURAA AARGH!!
NO! HE GOT HIT AGAIN!
NNNNGH!
DON'T WORRY. HE CAN ONLY DIE ONCE.
IT'S NOT OVER YET...!
I... DON'T WANT TO BE JUST A LAME CAT...
I WANT AMY TO SEE... WHAT I CAN DO!
NNNGH NNNGH
NNNGH
I BET YOU...
...THINK I'M LAME TOO...
!

NOT AT ALL.
I'M IMPRESSED!
YOU DON'T WANT TO GET BACK AT HER, YOU JUST WANT TO WORK HARD AND CHANGE HER MIND ABOUT YOU!
THAT'S REALLY AMAZING.
I DON'T UNDERSTAND WHY HE'D EVEN WANT TO SEE HER AFTER WHAT SHE SAID...
THAT'S EASY.
IT'S BECAUSE THIS CAT...
...TRULY LOVES AMY!

MEOW. ♪
GOOD LUCK, CAT!
...!
I'VE MET HUNDREDS OF YO-KAI...
...BUT EVERY ONE JUST MADE FUN OF ME.
THE ONLY ONE WHO HAS WISHED ME GOOD LUCK...
?

MEOW!
...WAS YOU! A HUMAN!!
REALLY? BUT IT'S SUCH AN ORDINARY THING TO SAY...
THANK YOU SO MUCH! I'M GOING TO KEEP WORKING HARD!
THE ONLY THING I REMEMBER FROM WHEN I WAS ALIVE IS AMY.
I DON'T EVEN REMEMBER MY NAME...
BUT THE OTHER YO-KAI ALL CALL ME JIBANYAN.
HI, JIBANYAN.
I'M NATE.

NATE ADAMS.
HI, NATE.
?
FSH
NICE TO MEET YOU!
VWNNNNNNNNNNN
?!

TUMP
WHAT'S THAT?!
BYE-BYE!
THESE YO-KAI ...
... AREN'T SCARY AT ALL!!
SO... WHAT'S THIS?
THAT IS A YO-KAI MEDAL !!
YO-KAI WILL GIVE THEM TO YOU WHEN THEY ACCEPT YOU AS THEIR FRIEND.
IT'S ALSO A BINDING CON-TRACT!
?

YOU JUST SIGNED A CONTRACT THAT LETS YOU SUMMON THAT YO-KAI WHENEVER YOU WANT...
...BY PLACING THAT MEDAL INSIDE YOUR YO-KAI WATCH.
SUM-MON THEM?
YUP! GIVE IT A TRY!
HERE GOES...
FUMP
FWIP
TEK
YO-KAI MEDAL, DO YOUR THING!
SHENK

RRRRNNNNNNN

LOOK !!

PAWS OF FURY!!
MRRRRR AAAOOW!
CHOOM CHOOM CHOOM
WHAAAAA?!
CHOOM CHOOM
KRA-DOOM
GRRRAAAAAGH!!
HUNH?
WHEN YOU SUMMON YO-KAI, THEY ARRIVE FROM WHATEVER THEY WERE JUST DOING... SO THIS SOMETIMES HAPPENS...
SORRY, I WAS FIGHTING ANOTHER CAR...
NNGH
NNGH
OF COURSE...

WOW!
AS YOU CAN SEE, THE YO-KAI YOU BEFRIENDED WILL COME TO HELP YOU WHEN YOU'RE IN TROUBLE.
I'M GOING TO MAKE TONS OF YO-KAI FRIENDS!
AND THAT WAS THE END OF MY ORDINARY DAYS!
NATE ADAMS' CURRENT NUMBER OF YO-KAI FRIENDS: 1

CHAPTER 2:
THE YO-KAI ODD COUPLE!
FEATURING HAPPIERE AND DISMARELDA
OOH. ♪ SO THIS IS YOUR HOME, NATE! ♪
HE DOESN'T THINK HE'S STAYING WITH ME... DOES HE?!
PLEASE, COME RIGHT IN! ♪
CAREFUL THOUGH! THERE'S A STEP! ♪
JUST PULL THE DOOR TO OPEN IT!
I KNOW, I LIVE HERE.
YOU'RE REALLY GETTING ON MY NERVES.

FWOOO--M
I'M HOME--!
WHOA! WHAT'S WITH THE GLOOMY VIBE IN HERE?
ISN'T THAT JUST LIKE YOU?!
ARE YOU KIDDING?! LOOK WHO'S TALKING!
MOM! DAD! WHAT'S GOING ON?!
GO TO YOUR ROOM, NATE!
WHOA.
WHAT ABOUT THE OTHER DAY?! YOU...
THAT HAS NOTHING TO DO WITH THIS!
...
TAP
!

KNOCK IT OFF! THEY'RE NOT USUALLY LIKE THIS! QUIT GIVING ME THAT LOOK!
THIS IS THE FIRST TIME I'VE EVER SEEN THEM FIGHT...
SEEING THEM LIKE THIS IS STARTING TO REALLY IRRITATE ME...
!!!
SO THAT'S WHY YOU WERE BEING SO HARSH WITH ME!
YOU TOLD ME I WAS GETTING ON YOUR NERVES!
WAP
YOU'VE BEEN GETTING ON MY NERVES FROM THE MOMENT WE MET!
OH STOPPIT.
HA HA HA HA HA.
WHY DOESN'T HE GET IT?!
!
YOU'LL FIND OUT WHY THEY'RE SO IRRITATED IF YOU JUST USE YOUR YO-KAI WATCH!
YOU MEAN ...
SCHIIIING...

FWAAAASH
WHOA!
NO! DON'T!
THIS IS THE REASON THEY'RE FIGHTING! MOM! DAD! STOP IT!
THEY STILL CAN'T SEE HER...
DWOOO~OO
DISMARELDA!! A YO-KAI WHOSE GLOOMY AURA INFECTS EVERYTHING AROUND HER, CAUSING TROUBLE BETWEEN ANYONE IN HER VICINITY!

DWOOOO...
AWW, WHAT'S THE POINT? IT'S ALL HOPE-LESS...
WHEN THAT YO-KAI IS AROUND, IT SAPS ALL YOUR MOTIVATION AND MAKES YOU FEEL IRRITATED!
NOW'S THE TIME TO USE YOUR YO-KAI MEDAL!
YOU'RE SUCH A PAIN IN THE NECK! WILL YOU SHUT UP ALREADY?!
SHUMP
AGH!
DID I SAY SOME-THING JUST NOW?
I KNOW YOU DIDN'T MEAN IT, BUT YOU SAID I WAS A PAIN IN THE NECK...
BECAUSE OF DISMER-ALDA!
WELL, I KIND OF MEANT IT BUT...
LET'S FIGHT FIRE WITH FIRE...I'M CALLING JIBANYAN!
YO-KAI MEDAL, DO YOUR THING!
CALLING...

JIBANYAN!
VRRRRRRRNNN
VNNNNNNNNNNNN
JIBAN-YAN! I NEED YOUR HELP!

THU
NGK
WHAT HAP-PENED?!
LOOKS LIKE HE LOST HIS FIGHT WITH A CAR.
OH NO! I'M SO SORRY TO SUMMON YOU AT A TIME LIKE THIS!
MEOW! OKAY!
VOOOSH
WHAT'S THE PROB-LEM? I'LL HANDLE IT!
DWOOOM
EHHH, NEVER MIND. WHAT'S THE POINT?
HE'S ALREADY LOST ALL HOPE!
VOOOSH
I'LL HAVE TO TAKE CARE OF IT MY-SELF!

BUT IT'S SUCH A PAIN... I DON'T WANT TO DO ANY-THING...
DWOOOOOM
DON'T YOU EVER LEARN?
WHO WANTS TO GET IN THE MIDDLE OF A LOVER'S QUARREL?!
JUST LOOK AT HOW NATE'S BEHAVING! IT'S ALL YOUR FAULT!
HE'S TALKING TO HIMSELF!
NO IT'S NOT! IT'S BECAUSE YOU'VE BEEN PAMPERING HIM!!
JIBA-NYAN, CAN YOU...
HUNH? JIBA-NYAN?
I'VE BROUGHT HELP!
SHUMP
?
HEY, WHERE HAVE YOU BEEN? I SUMMONED YOU TO COME HELP US, YOU KNOW!
DWOOM
DWOOM
I KNOW. IT'S OKAY. ♪
YOU'RE RIGHT! IT IS OKAY!
?
MEOW MEOW. ♪

THOOOM
SMILE!
HAPPI-ERRE!
OH! IT'S THAT NICE YO-KAI WE MET EARLIER! ♪
THOOOM
I DIDN'T BRING HAPPI-ERRE HERE TO FIGHT DISMAR-ELDA.
HE'S BEEN SEARCH-ING ALL MORN-ING...
I NOTICED HIM WHEN I WAS STANDING BY THE INTER-SECTION...
THAT'S IT! HE MIGHT BE ABLE TO DEFEAT DISMAR-ELDA!

...FOR HIS LADY!
I'VE BEEN LOOKING ALL OVER FOR YOU, DISMAR-ELDA.
COME TO THINK OF IT...
NOT OVER HERE. ♪
AND NOT OVER THERE. ♪
LOST! ♪ LOST!
THOOOM
I'M SORRY I LEFT YOU ALONE.
OH NO, IT'S MY FAULT. IT'S BECAUSE I'M SO SLOW.
THE VIBE IN HERE'S BACK TO NORMAL... I GUESS THE DOOM AND GLOOM AND HAPPINESS HAVE CANCELED EACH OTHER OUT!
YOU TWO KNOW EACH OTHER?
WE'RE...

...MARRIED.
BUT WE GOT SEPARATED DURING OUR WALK...
...BECAUSE I RUSHED TOO FAR AHEAD...
OH NO, IT'S BECAUSE I WAS TOO SLOW...
I CAME IN HERE LOOKING FOR MY HUSBAND...
I TRIED TO STOP YOUR PARENTS FROM FIGHTING BUT JUST ENDED UP MAKING IT WORSE... NO FILTER.
DWOOM
DWOOM
I SEE.
I MAKE PEOPLE SO HAPPY AND RELAXED THEY STOP WORKING...
AND SHE CAUSES TROUBLE BY MAKING PEOPLE UPSET.

WE BOTH CAUSE PROBLEMS WHEN WE'RE ALONE...
SO WE HAVE TO STAY TOGETHER ALL THE TIME!
BUT THAT'S...
...A GREAT THING FOR A HUSBAND AND WIFE, RIGHT?
IT REALLY IS! ♡
!
I THINK IT'S GREAT THAT YOU TWO WORK HARD TO HELP PEOPLE AS A COUPLE!
OH, BUT YOUR PARENTS ARE EVEN BETTER.
?

I'M SORRY... I TOOK THINGS TOO FAR.
SO DID I... I WAS JUST SO IRRITATED ...
I'M SORRY.
BEING ABLE TO APOLOGIZE TO EACH OTHER IS IMPORTANT. ♪
YEAH!

I DIDN'T KNOW THAT YO-KAI COULD BE TROUBLED BY THEIR POWERS.
...
WELL THEN. ALL'S WELL THAT ENDS WELL! WHAT'S NEXT? A BATH? DINNER?
HUNH HUNH
CHATTER CHATTER
OR HOW ABOUT THROWING ME A WELCOME PARTY?!
WHAT ABOUT THAT? HUH? HUH?
YAMMER YAMMER
WHAT A PAIN IN THE NECK!
UGH!
TEKT
YO-KAI MEDAL, DO YOUR THING!

I'M GLAD TO BE OF SERVICE! ♪
DWOO—OO
NEVER MIND... LET'S JUST GO TO BED.
NATE SUMMONED DISMARELDA WITH HER YO-KAI MEDAL.
DWOOO—OM
YOU CAN LET YOURSELF OUT.
PLEASE JUST CALL ANYTIME YOU--
...
WAAAUUUGH!
THERE, THERE!
BUT... BUT...!
NATE ADAMS' CURRENT NUMBER OF YO-KAI FRIENDS: 3

CHAPTER 3:
A YO-KAI FOOD FIGHT?!
FEATURING THE RICE CAKE YO-KAI
MOCHISMO

AAGGGH...
WOOOSH

I'M NATE ADAMS. AN ORDINARY ELEMENTARY SCHOOL STUDENT.
STOP!
OR I USED TO BE...
... BEFORE I MET THIS GUY.
HNNNGH!
IT IS MY FAULT AS YOUR BUTLER TO HAVE ALLOWED YOU TO OVER-SLEEP!!
HAVE NO FEAR! I WILL TAKE IT UPON MYSELF TO GET YOU TO SCHOOL ON TIME!!
NO! JUST STOP! PLEASE!
OH, DON'T WOR-RY ABOUT ME!
HNNNGH
I'M NOT WORRIED ABOUT YOU! THIS IS A...

...DEAD END!
KRA-THOOM
HUNH?!
NNNNGH!
HEFH... HEFH...
DINGDING
DINGDING
MADE IT...
THAT WAS CLOSE!
HEFH HEFH.
THIS IS WHISPER. HE'S A YO-KAI THAT ONLY I CAN SEE.
HEFH HEFH
NNGH
NNGH
SOMEONE LOCKED HIM INTO A STONE BALL BUT I FREED HIM.
BUT NATE...
SINCE THEN HE'S DECLARED HIMSELF MY BUTLER...
RRRMB
BLLEE
...THIS PLACE...
...LOOKS AWESOME! LOOK AT ALL THE PEOPLE! WOW!
VOOSH
LOOK OVER THERE! LOOK! LOOK! SEE?
...HE REALLY GETS ON MY NERVES...
WOW!
WOW!
WOW!
WOW!
WOW!
I KNOW. I COME HERE EVERY DAY...

GOOD MORNING.
5-2
DINGDING DINGDING
GOOD MORNING.
SLAM
OKAY, CLASS. ARE YOU READY FOR ME TO TAKE ATTENDANCE?
SORRY I'M LATE! HEFH HEFH.
HEFH
HEFH
YOU'RE TARDY AGAIN, EDDIE.
SORRY.
THAT'S TEN DAYS IN A ROW FOR YOU. EVERY DAY SINCE WINTER BREAK!
OVERSLEEP AGAIN, EDDIE?
NO, IT'S JUST THAT...
WHENEVER I CROSS THE ROAD IN FRONT OF MY HOUSE, MY FEET SUDDENLY BECOME SUPER HEAVY...
...AND IT TAKES FOREVER FOR ME TO GET ANYWHERE...

PSST PSST
WHISPER, DO YOU THINK...
YES, THERE'S NO DOUBT ABOUT IT.
I SUSPECT THAT IT HAS TO BE...
...SOME TYPE OF MYSTERIOUS ILLNESS THAT KEEPS MY BODY FROM MOVING!
AND IT'S CALLED THE I-DON'T-WANT-TO-GO-TO-SCHOOL FLU. ♪
HA HA HA HA HA HA
NO! IT'S NOT!
...

OF COURSE NO ONE BELIEVES ME...
...
I THINK IT'S WORTH INVESTI-GATING!
RIGHT!
TEKT

EDDIE. ♪
NATE.
TELL ME MORE ABOUT WHAT HAPPENS TO YOU IN THE MORNINGS!
YOU BELIEVE ME?!
OF COURSE!
MY MOM AND DAD DON'T EVEN THINK I'M TELLING THE TRUTH...
I'M SO HAPPY TO FIND SOMEONE WHO BELIEVES ME...
I BELIEVE YOU!
IT'S THE WORK OF A YO-KAI, THERE'S NO DOUBT ABOUT IT!
WOOOOSH
HUH?
YO-KAI DON'T EXIST.
GET REAL.
SHUMP SHUMP
ARE YOU KIDDING?! I WANT TO HELP YOU!
THIS IS THE ROAD WHERE IT HAPPENS?
YEAH, I START WALKING AND...
UNNGH!

NNNNNGH
HRRRRNGH
...
WHISPER, DO YOU SEE ANYTHING?!
NNNNGH. MAN...IT'S HAPPENING AGAIN... WHAT'S... GOING ON?!
GRRR RRN...
Y-YES... HE SEEMS TO BE TARGETING... ONLY EDDIE.
SHOW YOURSELF, YO-KAI!
FWAAASH
FWIP
KLIKT
GULP.
A YO-KAI THAT SHOCKS WHISPER... WHAT COULD IT BE...?

WHAAAM
HUFF HUFF
PLIPT PLIPT
WHAAAAT?!
THE YO-KAI WATCH: A WATCH THAT LETS YOU SEE YO-KAI THAT ARE INVISIBLE TO THE HUMAN EYE.
WHAT ...?
HUH? DID YOU SEE SOME-THING?
THEY'RE ONLY VISIBLE TO THOSE WEARING THE WATCH.
I-IT'S A RICE CAKE YO-KAI ...
RICE CAKE ?!
IT'S THROW-ING RICE CAKES UNDER EDDIE'S FEET TO MAKE IT HARDER FOR HIM TO WALK...
STRRRCH...
SHEF SHEF
HUFF HUFF
...
BUT... WHY?
HEY YOU ...
VNN-NN
!

VOOO—SH
RICE GUY! CAN YOU SEE ME?
JIGGLE
JIGGLE
IS THIS SOME KIND OF JOKE?!
PSSST PSSST
THIS ISN'T JUST SOME SILLY PRANK. I'M GETTING REVENGE...
...ON HIM.
JIGGLE
JIGGLE
I WAS BORN FROM THE RAGE OF ALL THE RICE CAKES THROWN AWAY WITHOUT BEING EATEN!
I'LL GLUE HIS FEET TO THE GROUND USING RICE CAKES TO SHOW HIM HOW VENGEFUL WE CAN BE!
ARE YOU SERIOUS?! THIS IS INSANE!
INSANE?!
RICE CAKE YO-KAI
MOCHISMO

HUFF HUFF
HOW RUDE!
I WILL EXACT MY REVENGE NO MATTER WHAT!
TUNK TUNK
NATE, THE IMPORTANT THING ABOUT YO-KAI WITH GRUDGES IS TO BE CAREFUL NOT TO MAKE THINGS WORSE.
OKAY!
I BET YOU DON'T EVEN LIKE EATING RICE CAKES DURING NEW YEAR'S FEAST!
AND YOU LIKE THE HERRING ROE AND CHESTNUT PASTE BETTER, DON'T YOU?!
WHAT IS HE TALKING ABOUT ...?!
YOU'RE JEALOUS OF THE NEW YEAR'S FOOD?!
HE'LL ONLY LET IT GO IF EDDIE LEARNS HIS LESSON AND APOLOGIZES!
NNNGH... WHY IS THIS HAPPENING ...?!
EDDIE, DID YOU THROW AWAY RICE CAKES DURING THE NEW YEAR'S CELEBRATION?
RICE CAKES? YEAH, I GOT TIRED OF EATING THEM. ♪
GRAAAAAAAH
HE'S MAKING IT WORSE!
BUT RICE CAKES ARE GOOD, AREN'T THEY?
SURE... AT FIRST.
BUT I GET TIRED OF EATING THEM PRETTY FAST.
HA HA HA ...

YOU UNGRATE-FUL BRAT!
GRAAAAH
AND RICE CAKES ARE ONLY GOOD FOR DURING NEW YEAR'S, SO AFTERWARD THEY'RE PRETTY MUCH USELESS.
AIIIEEEEEE!
I'LL NEVER FORGIVE THIS BOY!
GRRRRRR!
IT'S GETTING BIGGER... AND EVEN ANGRIER!
NATE... ARE YOU TALKING TO YOURSELF?
BE CAREFUL! WHO KNOWS WHAT IT WILL DO!
I HAVE TO GET EDDIE OUT OF HERE!
I'VE BEEN TOO EASY ON YOU... FROM NOW ON...
KRRRT
KRRRT

WHA
I
AAA
WHAT?! YOU THINK DOUBLE RICE CAKES IS CRAZY?!
THIS IS CRAZY!
Y-AAAAAAH!
I'LL THROW TWICE AS MANY RICE CAKES ON THE GROUND!
FSH FSH FSH
PLIP PLIP PLIP
SHUMP SHUMP
SHUMP SHUMP
THEN I'LL GLUE DOWN HIS ENTIRE BODY WITH A SUPERSIZED RICE CAKE!!
HUH?
EDDIE, RUN!!
VN
EAT THIS!
NNNNN

TUNK
BOOSH
SHUMP
BECAUSE I'M... THE ONLY ONE... WHO COULD... HELP HIM...
NNGH
NATE, WHY DID YOU SACRIFICE YOURSELF FOR EDDIE?!
IF YOU DON'T REMOVE IT QUICKLY, IT'LL TURN YOU INTO A RICE CAKE STATUE! ♪
GLOOOSH
HMMMGH. MMMFFH...
HRRRRNGH!
HNNNGH!!
FEAR NOT! I'LL HAVE IT OFF OF YOU IN NO TIME!
HIII-YA-YA-YA-YA!
THAT'S MY MASTER! WHAT A FINE YOUNG MAN!
HURRY UP AND HELP ME...
VSHVSH
VSH
VSH

SHLUNN—GK
UHH...?
WHAT...
I WASN'T EXPECTING THIS!
BE CAREFUL, NATE! THIS RICE CAKE IS SUPER STICKY!
I KNOW! THAT'S WHY WE'RE STUCK TOGETHER!
NOW TO SMOTHER HIM WITH GOOEY RICE CAKES!
EDDIE!
!!
I KNOW!
NNGH...

I'LL USE MY YO-KAI WATCH!
NNNGGH...
THAT'S IT!
YOU'RE GOING TO CALL HIM, AREN'T YOU?!
NNNGH...
THE MEDAL... IS IN... MY POCKET ... HNNNGH
HURRY! HE'S GETTING CLOSER!
I'M... TRYING...
HNNGH...
YO-KAI... MEDAL...
DO YOUR THING!

CALLING ...
VNNN
VRRRRRR
VRRRNNN
BY PLACING THE YO-KAI MEDAL IN THE YO-KAI WATCH, NATE CAN SUMMON THE YO-KAI HE'S BEFRIENDED.
VRRRN
!?
JIBANYAN!

HUNGRY!
TWITCH TWITCH
WHAT HAP-PENED ?!
JIBANYAN
I HAVEN'T FOUND ANYTHING TO EAT LATELY...
TIIING...
NNGH...
JIBANYAN, GET THIS RICE CAKE OFF US!
HUNH ?!
MRRAAOW!
OSH
VOO
WAIT! YOU CAN'T JUST DIVE IN OR YOU'LL GET STUCK IN IT TOO!

HE'S EATING IT!
NOM NOM NOMNOM NOMNOM NOM NOM
FOOOOD!
NOM NOM NOM NOM NOM NOM
BURRRRP
...
HOORAY! ♪
VOOSH
CHOOM CHOOM CHOOM CHOOM
ME-ME-ME-ME-MEOW!
IT'S JIBANYAN'S PAWS OF FURY!
CHOOM CHOOM
YOU CAN DO IT, JIBANYAN!

OM NOM NOM NOM
HE'S EATING THE RICE CAKE?!
NOM NOM
HOW HUNGRY IS HE?
SHUNGK
JIBAN-YAN!
...HAVE SOME MORE!
HERE...
STRETTTCH
ARRRRRGGH! IT'S TOO STICKY AND WON'T COME OFF MY HANDS!
HELP!
THIS IS BONKERS!

HOLD ON JIBANYAN, I'LL HELP YOU!
CHOMP CHOMP
EAT, WHISPER!
YES!
CHOMP
CHOMP
CHOMP
CHOMP
OM NOMNOMNOM
CHOMP
NOM NOM
MOCHISMO ...!!
THIS RICE CAKE ...
ERRRM ...
TWITCH TWITCH
HMNG ...
MMGH ...

SCH-FLI—ING
IS DELICIOUS!
THIS IS AMAZING! DO YOU HAVE ANY MORE?
WEIRD THING TO ASK SOME-ONE WE'RE FIGHTING BUT...
!!

OF COURSE THERE'S MORE!
WAAAA...
PHEW, I'M STUFFED! ♪
THANK YOU SO MUCH!
HUNH?
FSSS...
THANK YOU FOR EATING ME! ♪
OH... I SEE...

...
INSTEAD OF HOLDING A GRUDGE AGAINST EDDIE, WHY DON'T YOU HELP FEED THE HUNGRY?
...SO ITS GRUDGE DISAPPEARED ONCE WE ATE IT...
SNIFF
IT WAS BORN FROM A GRUDGE OVER NOT BEING EATEN...
HE TURNED BACK...
WHAAAM
YOU CAN HELP ANYONE WHO NEEDS YOU!
IT'S NOT JUST FOR THE HUMANS...
JIGGLE JIGGLE
I DON'T WANT TO HELP HUMANS WASTE MORE FOOD.
JIGGLE
I'M SURE ANYONE WHO EATS YOUR RICE CAKES WILL BE FILLED WITH ENERGY AND WARMTH!
THERE ARE HUNGRY YO-KAI TOO, RIGHT?
THIS ISN'T ABOUT HUMANS OR YO-KAI...

SCHIIIING
YOU REALLY THINK SO?
YEAH! I'M SURE OF IT!
JIGGLE
JIGGLE
I'LL GIVE IT A TRY! ♪
YEAH!
AND I WON'T PLAY TRICKS ON EDDIE ANYMORE!
CAN I EAT YOUR RICE CAKES AGAIN?
SURE. ♪
AND YOU'LL BECOME MY FRIEND SO I CAN SUMMON YOU LATER? ♪
OF COURSE. ♪
WHAT A GREAT PLAN...!
POP
ANOTHER YO-KAI MEDAL! THE SIGN OF OUR FRIEND-SHIP!
SHUMP...
HNGH ...?
OWW...

WHAT?! NOT AGAIN!
OH...
NNNGH... MY FEET... SO HEAVY...
MNNGH...
HE'S SO HAPPY ...
I'M GOING RIGHT HOME TO PLAY VIDEO GAMES! ♪
BYE!
MY FEET ARE BACK TO NORMAL! HOORAY!
VOOOSH...
...
FWU-MP
WHEEZEWHEEZE
...
HE ATE TOO MUCH RICE CAKE...
NATE ADAMS' CURRENT NUMBER OF YO-KAI FRIENDS: 4

THE YO-KAI WATCH'S FUNCTION

KRRRKT
YO-KAI MEDAL...
...DO YOUR THING!

VNNNN
OH NO! I PLACED A COIN IN BY MISTAKE!

VRRRNNN...
WHAT KIND OF YO-KAI IS GOING TO APPEAR NOW?!

POP
IT MADE CHANGE!

CHAPTER 4: REMEMBER NOT TO FORGET!

FEATURING MEMORY EATER YO-KAI WAZZAT

BZZZZT
BZZZZT
ZZZ... ZZZ...
NATE'S LUNCH MONEY
I'M NATE ADAMS, AN ORDINARY ELEMENTARY SCHOOL STUDENT.

THUNGK
HUNH ?!
THUNGK
THUNGK
THUNGK
GRAAAAGH!
WHAT ARE YOU DOING?!
THIS IS WHISPER ...

AND FOR SOME REASON... HE THINKS HE'S MY BUTLER.
WHOOSH
IT'S MY FAULT THAT YOU FORGOT TO BRING IT WITH YOU YESTERDAY!
I'M SO EMBARRASSED THAT YOU HAVE TO STICK YOUR LUNCH MONEY BAG TO YOUR HEAD BEFORE GOING TO SLEEP!
THUNGK THUNGK
I MUST REPENT!
DON'T WORRY! I'M PUTTING IT IN MY BAG RIGHT NOW!
SHUMP
NATE, YOU'RE GOING TO BE LATE FOR SCHOOL!
KRRRKT
I'M GOING!
NO ONE ELSE CAN SEE HIM.
THUNGK THUNGK
GOOD MORNING CLASS!
NATE, DID YOU REMEMBER YOUR LUNCH MONEY TODAY?
YES!
I HAVE IT RIGHT HERE IN MY BAG!
UHM ... ERM ...

I FORGOT MY BAG...
WHAAAAA
YOU'RE KIDDING ME!
I FORGOT MY FLUTE.
oh.
I FORGOT MY GYM CLOTHES...
I FORGOT MY TEXT-BOOKS...
I'M SUPPOSED TO BE YOUR BUTLER! IT'S ALL MY FAULT!
THUNGK THUNGK
WHAT'S GOING ON...? I FORGOT THE ATTEND-ANCE BOOK...
DING DONG
BRRRNT BRRRNT
I CAN'T BELIEVE I FOR-GOT MY BAG...
EVERY-ONE HERE SEEMS SO FOR-GET-FUL...
MAYBE THERE'S A YO-KAI IN THE CLASS-ROOM?!
FWIP
KLIKT
YO-KAI WATCH
A WATCH THAT HELPS YOU SEE THE YO-KAI AROUND YOU BY SHINING A SPECIAL LIGHT ON THEM.
FWAASH
MURMUR MURMUR
FWAASH FWAASH
MURMUR
WHISPER, DO YOU SEE ANYTHING?

HUNH?!
BWOOOM
AH-HA! YOU'RE WAZ-ZAT!
HO HO HO! ♪
I NEVER THOUGHT I'D MEET A HUMAN WHO CAN SEE US. ♪
MEMORY EATING YO-KAI WAZZAT
BE CAREFUL, NATE! THIS YO-KAI EATS PEOPLE'S MEMORIES!
THEIR MEMO-RIES?!
THE REASON WHISPER DIDN'T WARN ME ABOUT YOU...
...IS THAT YOU'VE AL-READY EATEN HIS MEMO-RIES ?!

WHA-WHA-WHA
WHAT? WHO'S GOING TO EAT WHAT NOW?
HO HO HO
HE'S DOING IT RIGHT NOW!

AH-HA! YOU'RE WAZ-ZAT!
BE CAREFUL, NATE! THIS YO-KAI EATS PEOPLE'S MEMORIES!
HE'S ALREADY FORGOT-TEN WHAT HE JUST SAID...
I'VE GOT IT!

SO YOU'RE THE ONE BEHIND EVERY-BODY'S FORGETFUL-NESS!
HO HO HO.
THAT'S RIGHT.
WHY ARE YOU DOING THIS?!
HO HO ...

A LONG TIME AGO... MY MASTER LEFT ME...
I WAITED FOR MY MASTER TO COME BACK, BUT...
...HE MUST HAVE FORGOT-TEN...

AND THAT'S WHY YOU'RE TRYING TO GET REVENGE ON EVERY-ONE?!
OH NO! I'M NOT TRYING TO GET REVENGE ON ANYONE!
I JUST ...

...WANT TO SEE PEOPLE PANIC BECAUSE I HAVE A GRUDGE AGAINST THEM!
BWO-OM
BUT THAT'S WHAT TRYING TO GET REVENGE MEANS!
NATE, WHAT ARE YOU MUMBLING ABOUT?
HEY, BEAR... IT'S NO-THING...
THE OTHERS CAN'T SEE IT...
NAME: BARNABY BERNSTEIN NICKNAME: BEAR
HEY, I'VE COME UP WITH A NEW PRANK. LET ME TRY IT OUT ON YOU.
TIIIING
NO!
I DON'T GET IT... WHY IS EVERYONE SAYING NO TO ME...?
WHAT'S NOT TO GET?!
OH! OUR TEACHER ASKED YOU TO COME TO THE FACULTY LOUNGE.
DON'T SAY I DIDN'T WARN YOU...
WHAT...? DID I DO SOMETHING WRONG?
MAYBE IT'S ABOUT YOUR LUNCH MONEY?
OH...
EXCUSE ME?
THEY'VE FOR-GOT-TEN ABOUT ME...
ZOOOSH

WHOA!
WHAT?! KOFF KOFF
BWAHAHAHA! THE BLACKBOARD ERASER BOMB WORKED!
BEAR, DID YOU DO THIS?!
WHAT IF I DID?!
YOU GOT A PROBLEM WITH IT?!
THEN WHY DON'T YOU JUST BEAT IT?!
UHH... NO, I DON'T...
WHO SHOULD I TAR-GET NEXT? ♪
YOU GOT A PROBLEM WITH IT?!
SO MEAN...
WHY DON'T YOU PLAY THE SAME PRANK ON HIM?
HE'D NEVER FALL FOR HIS OWN PRANK!
YOU REALLY THINK SO?
BEARS 90

HUNH? WHAT WAS I DOING JUST NOW?
BEAR, THE TEACHER WAS CALLING FOR YOU.
REALLY? ARE YOU SERIOUS?
I'LL GO RIGHT NOW!
ZOOSH
DID I DO SOMETHING WRONG?
THOOFH
GAHH!
YEAH!
HUNH?

THOOM
DID YOU DO THIS?!
HEY! YOU DID IT TOO!
MURMUR MURMUR
HUNH?!
WHAT HAPPENED?
OWW...
ARE YOU ALL RIGHT, NATE?
IT'S SO EMBARRASSING TO GET PUNCHED IN FRONT OF EVERYONE...
YOU WANT ME TO ERASE IT FROM PEOPLE'S MEMORIES?
...!!!

WHA
WHA
WHA
WHA
WHAT'S WRONG, NATE?
ARE YOU SICK OR SOME-THING?
WHAT'S GOING ON?
UH...
...
...
NATE, DID YOU BRING THE MANGA I LENT YOU?
OH...
YOU OWE ME A HUNDRED BUCKS IF YOU FORGOT AGAIN, REMEM-BER?
SHOOT! I TOTALLY FORGOT...!
HUNH?

W...
WHO DID I LEND IT TO...?
OR... DID I LEND IT TO SOMEONE ELSE?
THIS IS THE FIRST TIME ANYONE'S BEEN HAPPY WITH WHAT I'VE DONE!
SKOOSH
WOW...!
WOW! YOU'RE AMAZING!
COULD YOU HELP ME AGAIN?!
OF COURSE!
THIS IS NOT WHY I GAVE YOU THE YO-KAI WATCH!
HOW COULD YOU, NATE?!

AH-HA! YOU'RE WAZZAT!
VOOOSH
DO WE HAVE TO START FROM THERE AGAIN?
DINGDING
5-2
DINGDING
WE HAVE A TEST NEXT PERIOD, RIGHT?
MURMUR
MURMUR
UH-HUH, THE TEACHER TOLD US ABOUT IT LAST WEEK.
!!!
I TOTALLY FORGOT... I HAVEN'T EVEN STUDIED ...
TEST? WHAT TEST?
BUT YOU AN-NOUNCED IT LAST WEEK!!
YEAH!
WHAWHA
WHA
HUNH? HEY, WHAT'S WRONG?
?

BEAR, YOUR HEAD'S ALL WHITE!
NATE DROPPED THE BLACK-BOARD ERASER ON ME!
IS THAT TRUE, NATE?
NO, BEAR STARTED IT...
AND HE PUNCHED ME TOO!
RIGHT IN FRONT OF EVERY-ONE!
YOU SAW HIM PUNCH-ING ME, DIDN'T YOU?!
DID YOU?
I DON'T KNOW...
I FEEL SORRY FOR BEAR...
MAN UP AND APOLO-GIZE, NATE!
HOW COULD YOU BULLY BEAR LIKE THAT...?
YOU'RE AWFUL.
MURMUR MURMUR
OH NO ...I ERASED EVERY-ONE'S MEMORY OF IT...!

LIE?! ME...?!
YOU CAN'T LIE YOUR WAY OUT OF THINGS, NATE! I'LL SEE YOU IN MY OFFICE AFTER CLASS!
TEACHER'S OFFICE
NO MORE LYING, NATE! AND NO MORE PRANKS!
YES SIR...
CHEER UP, NATE.
DON'T LET IT GET YOU DOWN. WANT ME TO ERASE THIS MEMORY TOO?
NO, WE'VE ERASED ENOUGH. I DESERVE IT FOR TRYING TO TAKE THE EASY WAY OUT.
I ERASED THE MEMORIES OF PEOPLE WHO HAVE NOTHING TO DO WITH ANY OF THIS... JUST TO HELP MYSELF.
BUT YOU HAVEN'T DONE ANY-THING WRONG!
I'M SORRY, BUT I DON'T WANT TO RELY ON YOUR POWERS ANYMORE. I'M GOING TO APOLOGIZE TO THE OTHERS.
YOU TELL HIM!
HOW COULD YOU?!

BUT... BUT...
I THOUGHT YOU WERE SOME-ONE WHO NEEDED ME!
YOU'RE JUST GOING TO FORGET ME LIKE MY LAST MASTER!
YOU BETRAYED ME! I'LL ERASE YOUR ENTIRE MEMORY!
UH?! WHAT?!
NATE, RUN!

CHOMP
SHUT UP!
STOP IT, WAZZAT!
I'VE GOT IT!
TEKT
CHOMP CHOMP
YO-KAI MEDAL DO YOUR THING!
KRRRKT
VRRRRRRRN
CALLING ...
VOOOOOSH
JIBA-NYAN!

HI THERE.
JIBANYAN
WHAT ARE YOU WEARING?!
THIS IS MY COAT FOR WHEN IT GETS COLD.
I'M ACTUALLY QUITE A SNAZZY DRESSER, YOU KNOW.
OHHHH...
BUT NORMALLY YOU JUST WEAR A BELLY WARMER!
SHUMP
WOW! WHAT A FANCY HAT!
WHAT?!
HE PUT IT ON!

JIBANYAAAAAN!
WHERE AM I...? WHO AM I...?
NNNGH...
HO HO HO.
I'LL ERASE EVERYONE'S MEMORIES!
NNNN
GAAH!
NATE!
WHUMP
CHOMP
WHISPER!

!!!
WHAAAA
HE'S USING JIBANYAN AS A SHIELD!
SORRY, JIBANYAN !!

YAAAH!
SNAP
FWWW
AAARRRGH!
IIP
NO WAY...
WHIS-PER!
!!!
VOOSH
I WON'T LET YOU TOUCH NATE!
TWITCH
OWWW...
TWITCH

WHY YOU! THAT REALLY HURT!
OWW ...
I'M SORRY!
WHAA
IT WOKE UP.
SCHIING
CHOMP
CHOMP
EATEN.
OH...
...
JIBANYAAAN!
NNNGH...
SHUFF SHUFF
I...I'VE BEEN SAVED ...
THANK YOU, WAZZAT.
!

YOU... YOU'RE THE FIRST PERSON TO EVER TELL ME "THANK YOU"...
YUP YUP.
WELL, YOU DID HELP HIM AFTER ALL!
ME? HELP HIM?
SURE!
I THOUGHT THAT ALL MY POWERS WERE GOOD FOR WAS MAKING TROUBLE...
MAYBE I'VE BEEN USING THEM WRONG ALL ALONG...
I'M SORRY FOR CAUSING SO MUCH MIS-CHIEF...
WHAT ARE YOU TALK-ING ABOUT?
WE DON'T EVEN REMEM-BER.
YOU DON'T...?
HO HO HO...!
CALL ME WHEN-EVER YOU NEED MY HELP.
NNNNN...
FOR SURE! THANKS!
PLOP

NATE'S BEEN TALKING TO HIMSELF A LOT LATELY...
MURMUR
MURMUR
I GOT ANOTHER MEDAL!
YO-KAI CAN'T BE SEEN BY OTHER PEOPLE.
WHOOPS ... I'M STILL AT SCHOOL ...
LET'S NOT HANG OUT WITH HIM ANYMORE...
TOTALLY.
WHAT A FREAK.
HE'S A WEIRDO.
5-2
WHAAAAT?!
AGHH
WAZZAT! CAN YOU ERASE THEIR MEMORY JUST ONE MORE TIME?!
NOOOO!
SHUFF SHUFF
SHUFF SHUFF
...
NATE ADAMS' CURRENT NUMBER OF YO-KAI FRIENDS: 5

CHAPTER 5: DREAMS = DESIRE?!

FEATURING DREAM EATER YO-KAI BAKU

I'M NATE ADAMS.
RUMBLE...
NATE, IS EVERYTHING OKAY?
SLAAAAP
YAARRGH!!
HUUUNH?!
I HAVE A TEST TOMORROW.
OH! SO YOU'RE PSYCHING YOURSELF UP TO GET READY FOR IT?!
AN ORDINARY ELEMENTARY SCHOOL STUDENT.
NO...
TIIIING

CLI-KAT
I HAVEN'T STUDIED AT ALL, SO I HAVE TO PULL AN ALL-NIGHTER.
I WAS JUST TRYING TO SLAP MYSELF AWAKE.
IT'S TIME TO SUFFER THE CONSEQUENCES FOR ALL THE TIME YOU SPENT SLACKING OFF.
YOU DON'T HAVE TO BE SO BLUNT ABOUT IT.
SOMETIMES A BUTLER HAS TO SAY THE THINGS HIS MASTER DOESN'T WANT TO HEAR.
AND THIS IS WHISPER, A YO-KAI.
BUT I'LL STILL SUPPORT YOU NO MATTER WHAT!
TWEET TWEET TWEET
GO, NATE! GO!
VICTORY
SHUSH!
TWEET TWEET
HE DECLARED HIMSELF MY BUTLER FOR SOME REASON.
OKAY! NO SLEEP TONIGHT!
YAAAAH!
LET'S STUDY!
HMM...
...

ZZZZZZ... I DON'T... GET IT...

WHAAAAAAA

HE FELL ASLEEP IN TWO SECONDS!

BRRRNT
BRRRNT
GAAH, I FELL ASLEEP!
WHY DIDN'T YOU WAKE ME UP?!
IT'S IMPORTANT FOR GROWING CHILDREN TO GET THEIR REST!
I HAVE TO GET TO SCHOOL AND CRAM FOR THE TEST!
OH, IT'S BEAR!
NNGH NNGH
GOOD MORNING, BEAR!
NNNGH...
ZZZZ
WHAT?! HE'S SLEEP-WALKING!
HUH? OH! HI NATE. GOOD MORNING.
ARE YOU ALL RIGHT?
YEAH, I'VE JUST BEEN SO SLEEPY LATELY--
ZZZ...
GAAAH
HEY!

COME ON... WAKE UP...
ZZZ...
...
I HAVE TO GO STUDY...
NNGH NNGH
NNGH...
GOOD MORNING, CLASS.
GOOD MORNING!
5 - 2
AS DISCUSSED YESTERDAY, WE'LL BE HAVING A TEST.
NO! I DIDN'T HAVE ANY TIME TO STUDY!
SHUFL SHUFL
I DON'T EVEN UNDERSTAND THE FIRST QUESTION...
DINGDING DINGDING DINGDING
WAAH WAAH
BYE-BYE!
SEE YA!
LATER!
BEAR!
WOOOOSH

WHAT HAVE YOU GOT TO SAY FOR YOUR-SELF?!
...
YOU KEPT ME FROM STUDYING FOR THE TEST!
YOU DIDN'T DO WELL ON THE TEST, NATE...
...BECAUSE YOU FELL ASLEEP INSTEAD OF STUDYING.
WELL ...
HEY !!!
ZZZ ...
FWUMP
AND LOOK AT HOW SLEEPY BEAR IS!
DOESN'T THAT STRIKE YOU AS ODD?!
YOU'RE RIGHT!
KLIKT
FWIP
FWAASH
A YO-KAI!
YO-KAI WATCH SHINES A SPECIAL LIGHT THAT MAKES YO-KAI VISIBLE.

SUPER BEAR-MAN TO THE RESCUE!
WHA
AAM
WHAT?!
HUFF HUFF
HALT, MONSTER! YOU'LL HAVE TO DEAL WITH ME FIRST!
ZZZZ...
GRRRRR !!
THIS... MUST BE BEAR'S DREAM...
HIS DREAM? WHY DO WE SEE HIS DREAM AND NOT THE YO-KAI?
TAKE THIS: BEAR RAY!
BZZZZZ
GRAAAAAH!
ZZZ ZZZ...
TUMP TUMPTUMP
WHAT'S THAT?!
CHUKT

OM NOM NOM
I MUST PROTECT THIS PLANET FROM EVIL!
IT'S EATING BEAR'S DREAM!
HMPH...
MUNCH MUNCH
CHOMP CHOMP
FWUMP
WHISPER?!
?

ZZZ...
HUNH
HE'S JUST SLEEPING?!
A SLEEPING YO-KAI?!
HEH HEH HEH.
DID YOU MAKE BEAR FALL ASLEEP TOO?!
WHAT DO YOU WANT?!
WHAT DO I WANT?
I FEED ON PEOPLE'S DREAMS!
SO I MAKE THEM FALL ASLEEP AND DEVOUR THEIR DREAMS!
THE DREAMS OF HIGH-ENERGY PEOPLE LIKE HIM ARE PARTICULARLY GOOD.
...
HAVE YOU EVER...

...WOKEN UP IN THE MORNING, BUT BEEN UNABLE TO REMEMBER THE DREAM YOU JUST HAD?
WHHAAM
THAT'S BECAUSE I ATE IT!
DREAM EATING YO-KAI BAKU
ZZZ... ZZZ...
PUFF PUFF
!!
I'M WHISPER.
TO THANK YOU FOR RELEASING ME, I WILL BECOME YOUR PERSONAL BUTLER!
PUFF PUFF
HE'S DREAMING OF THE FIRST TIME WE MET...?!

HOW DO YOU DO. ♪
BAAAM
WHY DOES HE LOOK SO COOL?!
HE'S BUILT LIKE A MODEL!
BOUNCE BOUNCE
AND I'M A LITTLE STICK FIGURE!
PEOPLE'S DREAMS REVEAL THEIR TRUE NATURE...
...BUT THEY'RE ALL SO BORING.
I'M JUST TRYING TO FIND THE HUMAN WITH THAT ONE DREAM I'M LOOKING FOR.
SHE'S... LOOKING FOR A SPECIFIC DREAM?!

FRIEND?
I'M NOT TRYING TO CAPTURE YOU. I JUST WANT TO BE YOUR FRIEND...
HUMANS LOVE TO CAPTURE RARE BREEDS SUCH AS MYSELF!
HUFF
AND UNTIL THEN, I CAN'T ALLOW MYSELF TO BE CAPTURED!
?!
PWOOF
I WON'T FALL FOR THAT! SLEEPY SMOKE!
HUNH ...? OH ...
GET OUT OF THE WAY! IF IT HITS YOU, YOU'LL FALL ASLEEP!
WHAT ?!
SHUFF
IT'S WHAT MADE ME FALL ASLEEP!
FWUMP
THEN ...!
FWOOSH

YOU'RE THE ONE WHO MADE ME FALL ASLEEP WHEN I WAS STUDYING LAST NIGHT!
HUH? I'VE NEVER EVEN SEEN YOU BEFORE TODAY!
...
THEN...
YOU JUST FELL ASLEEP BECAUSE YOU'RE LAZY AND CAN'T CONCENTRATE.
I GUESS THERE'S NO REAL HARM IN FALLING ASLEEP AND LETTING HER EAT OUR DREAMS...
YOU'RE RIGHT. THERE'S NO REASON FOR US TO FIGHT IT...
YES, GO TO SLEEP...

DWOOOOF
WHOA!
... FOREVER!
VOOOOSH
FOR-EVER?!
IF YOU WANT TO DO THIS THE HARD WAY, THAT'S FINE BY ME!
YO-KAI MEDAL, DO YOUR THING!
KRRKT
CALL-ING...
VNN
JIBA-NYAN!!
VRRRRRR
NN
VRRR
RNNRR

YOU... CALLED ...?
PHEW ...
HOLD ON...
POOF
{HKKH} {HKKH}
NONONO! STAY IN BED! I'M SORRY!
YOU WANT ME... TO BEAT... THIS YO-KAI?
NO, IT'S FINE! YOU NEED YOUR REST!
NNNGH...
...
DON'T WORRY--
AHHH...
ACHOOO!
IF YOU'RE SICK, YOU SHOULD SLEEP!
PWOOH
JIBAN-YAN! RUN!
SHUFF
WHOA! HE DODGED IT!!

HE MUST HAVE COLLAPSED FROM EXHAUSTION!
FWOOOSH
SHLUMP
WHEEZE WHEEZE
TWITCH TWITCH...
WOW
I'M JIBA-NYAN.
I GOT INTO A FIGHT WITH A CAR.
HUFF HUFF
MY SLEEPY SMOKE MISSED BUT HE STILL FELL ASLEEP!
!!

MY DREAM IS TO BECOME A CAT WHO CAN BEAT UP CARS. ♪
SCHIING
HE LOOKS LIKE A MODEL TOO!
ALL THE OTHER YO-KAI MAKE FUN OF ME FOR IT.
SO STUPID! YOU'LL NEVER BEAT UP A CAR!
STUPID!
STUPID!
STUPID!
BUT THERE'S ONE PER-SON...
...WHO TOLD ME, "YOU CAN DO IT." A HUMAN.
SO I SWORE TO PROTECT HIM WITH MY LIFE...
YOU CAN DO IT!
HIS NAME IS NATE... I'LL NEVER FORGET THE DAY I MET HIM!
JIBA-NYAN...

I CAN'T BELIEVE THAT THERE'S A HUMAN WILLING TO BEFRIEND YO-KAI!
HEY!!
FOOFH
FOOFH
FOOFH
I CAN'T REMEMBER HIS FACE, THOUGH.
HMM...
THIS SOUNDS MORE LIKE A MEMORY THAN A DREAM.
THAT'S THE HUMAN!
NO, IT'S OKAY! GO BACK TO SLEEP!
WOBBLE WOBBLE
I'LL PROTECT YOU... NATE...
NNGH
NNGH...
SHUFF...
URGH...
...
I WON'T LET YOU LAY A FINGER ON--
AHHH...
STAND ASIDE! I CAN TELL WHAT TYPE OF PERSON SOMEONE IS FROM LOOKING AT THEIR DREAM!
FWOOFH
YOU'VE BEEN DECEIVED BY HIM!

FWOSH
ACHOO!!!
BOOOSH
AAARGH!!!
FWUMP
ZZZ
FWUMP...
JIBAN-YAN!
PUFF PUFF
OH... THE DREAM...

WHAAAT?!

WELL THEN, TIME TO GO EAT DREAMS AGAIN.
SCHIIING
YOU TOO ?!
I CAN'T LET THEM SLEEP ON THE ROAD, SO I'LL TAKE THEM HOME WITH ME...
...
MY MASTER IS SUCH A KIND YOUNG MAN. BAKU WAS OUR ENEMY JUST A MOMENT AGO, BUT HE'S STILL LOOKING OUT FOR HER.
SIGH ...
HUNH ?

TUMP
TUMP
ZZZ...
WHAAAAT?
HE ABANDONED BEAR!
HUNH?!
BLINK
HE WOKE UP!
ARE YOU ALL RIGHT?
WHY DIDN'T YOU KILL ME IN MY SLEEP?!
HUFF
NNGH
WHAT?! I'D NEVER DO THAT!
I WANTED TO DESTROY HIM, BUT HE LET ME SLEEP IN HIS BED...
MAYBE THAT CAT IS RIGHT... MAYBE THIS GUY REALLY IS...
I'VE WATCHED HUMANITY FOR THOUSANDS OF YEARS.
?
...
SINCE TIME IMMEMORIAL, HUMANS HAVE BLAMED EVERYTHING ON YO-KAI. CAPTURING, RESEARCHING AND EXTERMINATING US!
AS THE YEARS WORE ON, YO-KAI SLOWLY BECAME INVISIBLE TO HUMANITY.

MY DREAM IS FOR HUMANITY AND YO-KAI TO WORK TOGETHER AND COEXIST!
AND I'VE BEEN SEARCHING FOR A HUMAN WHO SHARES THE SAME DREAM!
SO THAT'S THE DREAM SHE WAS LOOKING FOR...
I DON'T KNOW IF I FULLY UNDER-STAND, BUT...
?
...I WANT ALL YO-KAI AND HUMANS TO BE FRIENDS! ♪
IF ONLY ALL HUMANS WERE LIKE THIS BOY...
...
NATE ...

WE'LL MEET AGAIN.
VNNN...
YOU'RE GOING TO BE MY FRIEND?! ♪
POP
ANOTHER YO-KAI MEDAL! THE SIGN OF OUR FRIENDSHIP!
I'M SO TIRED ...
CAN I HELP YOU GET TO SLEEP?
HA HA HA, THAT SOUNDS LIKE A GOOD IDEA. ♪
I'VE GRADED YESTER-DAY'S TESTS!
OH NO... I DON'T WANT TO SEE...
YOU DID REALLY WELL THIS TIME, NATE.
WHAT?!
MATH TEST
CLASS 5-2
NAME:
NATE ADAMS
QUESTION

NATE ADAMS' CURRENT NUMBER OF YO-KAI FRIENDS: 6

HOW TO USE THE YO-KAI MEDAL

CHAPTER 6: NATE'S LUCKY DAY

FEATURING LUCKY YO-KAI NOKO

HURRY!

WOOOOSH
LET'S GO!
I'LL GET TO THE BOOK-STORE IN NO TIME!
I'M NATE ADAMS.
I'M HAPPY TO HELP! ♪
HOLD ON TIGHT!
VNNN

HNNGH!
HUNH?
THUNGKT
VOOOOOSH
AN ORDINARY ELEMENTARY SCHOOL STUDENT.
AAAAAGH!!
P-TANNNG

UNNNGH...
I'M SO SORRY, NATE!
TWITCH TWITCH...
SHUNGK
NO!
TINK TINK
GAAAAH!
THUNGK
TINK TINK...
MY MONEY!

WHAA-AA
I WAS GOING TO USE THAT TO BUY A COROCORO COMIC!
HA HA HA ...
WHAAAM
SOME-THING ELSE I CAN HELP YOU WITH! ♪
SHWOOOP
HMM ...
OOOH, COOL.
OH ?!
DID YOU FIND IT?!
NO.
SHWOOOP...
IT'S TOO DARK FOR ME TO SEE ANY-THING.
AND THIS IS WHISPER, A YO-KAI...
OF COURSE ...
SHUMP

THIS IS SO UPSET-TING...
SHOOMP
STRETCHED!
ARE YOU OKAY ?!
I'M SORRY I COULDN'T HELP.
BOW
BONK
OW!
AND HE THINKS HE'S MY BUTLER FOR SOME REASON.
I'VE HEARD THERE'S A THIEF IN THIS NEIGHBOR-HOOD!
WHAAA...
HOW AWFUL!
NO ONE ELSE CAN SEE HIM.
A THIEF, HUH... ALL I HAVE IS ONE COIN, SO I'M NOT MUCH OF A TARGET...
!!
HUNH

FWAAASH
YO-KAI WATCH!
YO-KAI WATCH
SHINES A SPECIAL LIGHT THAT MAKES YO-KAI VISIBLE.
WHAT'S WRONG? DO YOU SUSPECT A YO-KAI IS AROUND?
FWAAASH
FWAAASH
MAYBE A YO-KAI HAS BEEN GIVING ME BAD LUCK!
I DON'T SEE ANYTHING...
SHUMP
SHUMP
I GUESS YOU'RE JUST UNLUCKY.
MAYBE THERE'S A COIN ON THE GROUND ...?
FWAAASH
DON'T USE THE YO-KAI WATCH AS A FLASHLIGHT!
NOOO!
HUNH ...?!
WHAT IS IT? DID YOU FIND A COIN?!
NO ...

WHAA—AM
SOME-ONE'S STUCK UNDER THERE!
ARE YOU OKAY? I'LL GET YOU OUT!
NRRRG...
KWEEE!
KWEEE!
JUST... HANG... IN THERE!
NNNGH
...
UH, NATE... HE'S ACTU-ALLY SPEAK-ING...
?

HUH!
I'VE BEEN CAUGHT BY A HUMAN!
GET YOUR FILTHY HANDS OFF ME, HUMAN SCUM! DROP DEAD!
THAT'S WHAT HE JUST SAID.
THAT'S SO RUDE!
SERIOUSLY?!
WHAAAAA
KWEEE!
PHEW... FINALLY.
DON'T WORRY, HE'S NOT A BAD GUY.
KWEE.
OH... THIS IS...
FWAAAASH
NOKO!
KWEE.
THIS YO-KAI BRINGS GOOD LUCK WHENEVER HE'S AROUND!
THIS IS AN EXTREMELY RARE TYPE OF YO-KAI.
LUCK YO-KAI NOKO
WOW! MAYBE NOW I'LL FIND A TON OF CASH!
KWEEE.
THE PITIFUL DREAM OF A PITIFUL HUMAN BEING... (SIGH)
HE SAID.
WHY'S HE SO NEGA-TIVE...?!
HE'S SO..
BRING IT ON!
YOU ASKED FOR IT!

CUTE! ♪
VOOSH
THU
NG
KT
?
A BASEBALL! IT WOULD HAVE NAILED YOU IF YOU'D BEEN STANDING UP! LOOKS LIKE YOUR LUCK IS ALREADY KICKING IN!
CRUMBLE...
SO DANGEROUS...
I'M SORRY!
BE CAREFUL!
HEY, NATE!
YOU WANT THIS?
THAT VIDEO GAME JUST CAME OUT!
MY DAD GOT IT FOR ME, BUT I ALREADY HAVE IT...
BYE!
WOW. THANKS!
NOKO... ♪ YOU'RE AMAZING!

WHAT HAP-PENED TO YOU?!
NNNGH...
TWITCH
TWITCH

KWEEEE, KWEEEE...
GIVING LUCK TO OTHER PEOPLE CAUSES HIM TO WASTE AWAY!
WHAAAAAT?!
HOLD ON A MIN-UTE!
EXCUSE ME! I NEED TO BUY THIS! FAST!
SURE. THAT'LL BE ONE COIN.
TER BAKERY
WHAT ...?

!!
EAT THIS!
RED BEAN BUN
...
GO AHEAD AND EAT! ♪
I FELT SO SORRY FOR HIM BEING SO SKINNY AND WEAK.
!!!
IT WAS ALL YOU HAD!
NATE... YOU USED ALL OF YOUR MONEY ON THAT!
WHAT'S WRONG? DOES HE FEEL GUILTY?
NO.
WHAT?!
DON'T SAY THAT! JUST EAT IT!
KWEEE-KWEE.

HE'D RATHER HAVE A RICE BALL THAN THE BUN.
KWEEE.
WHAAAAT?!
MUNCH MUNCH
SHWEEE
HE'S STILL CUTE THOUGH.
KWEE KWEE.
HMM.
IS HE COM-PLAINING AGAIN?
YOU'RE THE FIRST HUMAN WHO HASN'T TRIED TO CAPTURE HIM.
?

EVERYONE HE MEETS TRIES TO CATCH HIM FOR HIS GOOD LUCK...
HE GOT STUCK UNDER THE VENDING MACHINE WHILE TRYING TO RUN AWAY FROM A HUMAN.
I DON'T WANT HIM TO THINK I'M JUST AFTER HIS GOOD LUCK...
...SO IT'S AWKWARD TO ASK HIM TO BE MY FRIEND...
?
MAYBE I WON'T!
!
NATE ISN'T GREEDY AT ALL! NOKO'S SURE TO BECOME HIS FRIEND NOW! HE JUST NEEDS TO ASK!
HUNH?
COROCORO
VOOOSH
A COMIC! ON THE GROUND?!
COROCORO
AND IT'S THE NEWEST ISSUE TOO!
SQUEE.
YOU'RE SO LUCKY, NATE!

A COROCORO COMIC...
SIGH...
COROCORO
WHY COULDN'T IT BE MONEY?
YOU'RE COM-PLAINING NOW ?!
EEEEK!! HE'S A THIEF! STOP HIM!
!!!
WOOOSH
GET OUT OF MY WAY!
HELP!
HUNH ?!

THUNGK
UNGH!
WHOA!
RUNNING INTO A THIEF ISN'T EXACTLY LUCKY...
NNGH
NOKO'S POWER IS INCREDI-BLE. ♪
I WAS LUCKY... THAT WAS SUPER CLOSE!
FWUMP
OH, I'M SO SORRY!
AGGH!
TUNK
KWEEEE
WHOA!
FWSH
FWSH
FWSH
I SAID GET OUT OF MY WAY!

WHOA!
SWWWISH
SWOOSH
SWUP

NATE!

THAT WAS CLOSE ...!
SO LUCKY.
COROCORO
TUG
THE COMIC?!
IT SAVED HIS LIFE...
TUNK
TUNK-TUNK
THAT'S HIM, OFFICER!
NNGH!
VOOOOSH
FWOSH
GET BACK HERE!
COROCORO COMICS ARE THICK SO THEY HURT A LOT!

KWEEEO
WHERE WERE YOU AIMING?!
WHOOPS ...
FWOOOOO
TUNK TUNK TUNK
THWUNK
THOOM
VRRRRM
GRRRRN
OOO
CORO CORO

UNNNGH...!!
KRUNCH
PA-TANG!
GORO
COROCORO
WHAAAM
NO WAY! IT'S BECAUSE OF NOKO'S LUCK!
JUST LIKE I PLANNED!
WOW! GREAT JOB, NATE!
NNNNGH...
YEAH...

HEY, MISTER ...
LUCKY FOR ME, I HAVE YO-KAI FRIENDS!
THANK YOU SO MUCH! ALL OF MY MONEY WAS IN THAT BAG!
WELL DONE.
THANKS, NOKO! YOU SAVED THE DAY! ♪
HE WANTED TO THANK YOU FOR SPENDING ALL YOUR MONEY ON FOOD FOR HIM TO EAT.
KWEEE ...
I'M GLAD YOU LIKED IT.
KWEE.
AND NOW HE'D LIKE YOU TO BE HIS FRIEND.
OH! OF COURSE!

ANOTHER YO-KAI MEDAL! THE SIGN OF OUR FRIENDSHIP!
PO
PT
I KNOW! ♪
I'M SO LUCKY TO HAVE MET HIM! ♪
WITH NOKO AS MY FRIEND, I'VE GOT NOTHING TO WORRY ABOUT!
NATE!
BUT... NOKO...? WHERE'S ...YOUR LUCK...?
THUNK
UNGH!!

NNN-GH...
HE WITHERS AWAY AS HE GIVES PEOPLE LUCK...
WHEN HE'S REALLY LOW ON ENERGY, HE LOSES HIS LUCK ALTO-GETHER!
SO THAT'S THEM...

BZZZ...
THEY'RE THE ONES TRICKING YO-KAI INTO BECOMING THEIR FRIENDS!
WHAAAM
UNFOR-GIVABLE...
SQUEE...
NATE ADAMS' CURRENT NUMBER OF YO-KAI FRIENDS: 7

CHAPTER 7: TURN THAT FROWN UPSIDE DOWN!

FEATURING YO-KAI NEGATIBUZZ

HEY, WHISPER. LET'S TAKE A LITTLE BREAK FROM THE YO-KAI SEARCH. ♪
THANKS SO MUCH! ♪
PSSH
I'M NATE ADAMS...
...AN ORDINARY ELEMENTARY SCHOOL STUDENT.
GULP
JUST A MINUTE, NATE!
HUNH?
H
MY HEAD GOT STUCK...! HELP ME...!
AGHH!

Every Day
BUT HOW...?!
FOO
SHUFF
SHUFF
SHUFF
SHUFF

NNNNGH...
OWWW!
THIS IS WHISPER, A YO-KAI.
HEFH HEFH
EVEN THE AUTOMATIC DOOR SENSORS DON'T NOTICE ME...
ARE YOU OKAY?
FOR SOME REASON, HE'S MADE HIMSELF MY BUTLER.
ALL RIGHT... LET'S GO SEARCH FOR YO-KAI!
YEEAAH!
LET'S ASK SOMEONE TO HELP US! ♪
I HAVE SO MANY FRIENDS NOW!
MAYBE NOKO? BUT HE GETS WORN OUT SO QUICKLY...
LET'S CALL JIBANYAN!
VOOOSH

YO-KAI WATCH!
YO-KAI WATCH
ALLOWS YOU TO SUMMON THE YO-KAI YOU'VE BEFRIENDED.
YO-KAI MEDAL, DO YOUR THING!
FWIPT
CALLING ...
COME ON OUT...
VNN
NN
HUP!
JIBAN ...
WHAT DID YOU DO THAT FOR?!
DON'T WORRY, I CAN HANDLE THINGS WITHOUT HIM.
BUT IT'D BE SO MUCH EASIER TO SEARCH IF THERE WERE MORE OF US!
HUNH ?!

OH NO!
WHA—AAA
TWITCH
TWITCH
TWITCH
JIBANYAN WAS ALREADY HALFWAY OUT!
SO SORRY!

BLABBER
BLABBER
NNNNNNNN
BLABBER
BLABBER
I'M ALL YOU REALLY NEED FOR THE YO-KAI SEARCH ANYWAY!
MY JOB AS YOUR BUTLER IS TO ENSURE YOU BEFRIEND YO-KAI AS SMOOTHLY, ENJOYABLY AND SAFELY AS POSSIBLE!
BUT WON'T IT BE FASTER IF WE--
THERE'S NO NEED!
THE WORLD'S SWARMING WITH YO-KAI, SO FINDING THEM COULDN'T BE EASIER. HA HA HA! LET'S GO! ♪
...
BLABBER
BLABBER
BLABBER
I THINK YOU'RE BEING OVER-CONFIDENT.
AND YOU'RE BEING TOO NEGATIVE, NATE!
YAMMER YAMMER
YAMMER
OH, DO YOU KNOW WHAT NEGATIVE MEANS? ♪
IT'S TO BE SKEPTICAL AND LOOK AT THINGS FROM A BAD ANGLE.
BY THE WAY, DO YOU KNOW WHAT THE OPPOSITE OF BEING NEGATIVE IS? IT'S BEING POSITIVE! ♪
UGH! SO ANNOYING!
YAMMER YAMMER
WHO IS?
HUH?
YOU! WHY CAN'T YOU JUST CALM DOWN?!
JERK!
NEVER MIND THAT. LET'S GO SEARCH FOR YO-KAI!
HUMPH...
FWAASH
WE'LL NEVER FIND A YO-KAI THIS EASILY...
HUNH?
YOU CAN SEARCH FOR YO-KAI WITH THE YO-KAI WATCH'S SPECIAL LIGHT!

FWA
I FOUND ONE! IT'S A PITCH-BLACK YO-KAI!
MUMBLE MUMBLE ...
AASH
RRUMBBLEE
NO, THERE'S NO SUCH THING!!
THAT'S JUST A HUMAN!
I'M NO GOOD... JUST PLAIN NO GOOD... NO GOOD AT ALL...
ZWOOM
IT'S OVER... I'M DONE FOR... MY LIFE WAS OVER BEFORE IT BEGAN...
WHAT HAP-PENED?
VWOOO-SH
HA HA HA ... WHAT HAP-PENED ?!

HA HA HA HA! NOTHING HAPPENED! I'VE GOT NOTHING! NO SKILLS, NO FRIENDS AND NO MONEY!
SHLUMP
I'M DONE FOR! HA HA HA HA HA!
WHOA... WHAT DID I GET US INTO...?
HE'S A VERY NEGATIVE PERSON...
I'M SURE THINGS WILL GET BET-TER...
HUH?
MY LIFE COULD GET EVEN WORSE, YOU KNOW? WHY WOULD YOU THINK IT WILL IMPROVE?!
NNNNGH
WHAT CAN I EVEN DO ABOUT THIS?!
YO-KAI MEDAL DO YOUR THING!
KRRRKT
CALLING ...
VNNNNNN

HAPPIERRE!
SMILE! ♪
NNNNNNNNN
HA HA HA HA HA HA HA HA HA...
BUMP-A BUMP-A BUMP-A
BUMP-A BUM
TWEEEET
SMILE! ♪
HUNH ...?
I'M COUNTING ON YOU. ♪
"HAPPIERRE?" WHAT'S THAT EVEN MEAN...?
WHY AM I EVEN TALKING TO THIS KID?
YO-KAI CAN ONLY BE SEEN BY PEOPLE WHO HAVE THE YO-KAI WATCH.

AHHHHHH
WHY WAS I SO DEPRESSED?!
HAPPIERRE
A YO-KAI THAT MAKES PEOPLE HAPPY AND RELAXED.
ALL THE TIME I SPENT GETTING HIM DOWN... WASTED!
SHUF SHUF
HAPPY! ♪
WELL DONE, HAP-PIERRE! ♪
I'M SO GLAD!
I FEEL SO LIGHT! ♪
BZZ
HAHAHAHAHA!
FWSH
BZZZZZZ
?!
CAREFUL! I SENSE A YO-KAI IN THE AREA!
HE'S GOT... WINGS?!
TUMP
TUMP

THUNGK
GAAAAH!
...
NO! THAT WAS MY BEST CHANCE OF BEATING THEM AND IT FAILED! I'M FINISHED!
I SHOULD CALL MYSELF THE BUMBLING BUZZ...
DRAT!
WHAT'S... GOING ON...?
...
I KNOW! YOU'RE WHY THAT GUY WAS ACTING SO STRANGE!
WHAAAA
HOW DID YOU KNOW ?!
HE MUST BE A NEGATIVE YO-KAI!
HUUUNH?!
YOU FIGURED THAT OUT TOO?!
THEN THAT MUST MEAN ...

YOU ALREADY KNOW ABOUT MY PLAN TO TURN EVERY HUMAN NEGATIVE SO THAT THE ENTIRE WORLD BECOMES DARK AND GLOOMY?!
WHAAA!
AAA
NO WAY!
WE DIDN'T KNOW ANY OF THAT!
WOW.
THIS YO-KAI IS SO PESSI-MISTIC.
OH GREAT! I'M GLAD IT'S STILL A SECRET.
PHEW, THAT WAS CLOSE!
HE MUST BE A LITTLE SLOW...
NEGATIVE YO-KAI
NEGATIBUZZ
YOU GIVE PEOPLE NEGATIVE PERSONALITIES? THEN IS THAT MAN ANOTHER VICTIM?!
HA HA, NO... THIS GUY...
THIS KID'S PICKING A FIGHT WITH ME...
...WAS NATURALLY NEGA-TIVE TO BEGIN WITH!
NEGATIVE PEOPLE ARE WONDER-FUL SOURCES OF ENERGY FOR ME.
YOU FEED OFF NEGA-TIVE FEEL-INGS?
YES.
EVEN CHILDREN MAKE FUN OF ME. WHAT A MISERABLE LIFE...

NEGATIVE PEOPLE CARRY AROUND NEGATIVITY GERMS, AND I...
SMILE! ♪
FWOO-SH
OH MY! WHY WAS I SO WORKED UP OVER NOTHING?!
AHHHH
HEY!!!
LA LA LA LA LA. ♪
AHH-H
TAKE CARE!
FWUMP...
SMILE! ♪
?
PAT
HE WAS MY STEADY SOURCE OF NUTRITION... AND YOU LET HIM GO JUST LIKE THAT...?!
UGGGGN...
I EVEN HAD HIM STAND WITH ME IN THE LAST CHAPTER TO MAKE ME LOOK MYSTERIOUS...
IT'S ALL OVER. I'M DONE FOR...

HA HA HA HA! ♪
BZZZZ
BUT THE WORLD IS FULL OF NEGATIVE PEOPLE! ♪
I CAN ALWAYS LOOK FOR SOMEONE ELSE TO FEED OFF OF! ♪
YOU EVEN MADE OUR ENEMY HAPPY! WHAT ARE YOU DOING, HAPPIERRE?!
VWOOOSH
SORRY! ♪
YOU CERTAINLY DON'T LOOK SORRY!
NYAHAHAHA!
TAKE THIS! NEGATIVITY GERMS!
FUMPT
WHOA!
THWK
NATE, LOOK OUT!

KRA-THOOM
GAAAAH!
NO
NO
NO
NO
NO!
TWITCH TWITCH
I'M SO SORRY!
VSH VSH VSH
SHUNGK
I... I'M FINE...
NO YOU'RE NOT!
THUD THUD
I BET YOU'RE FURIOUS! YOU TOTALLY ARE! AGGH, HE HATES ME!
WHAT'S GOING ON?!
IT MUST BE BECAUSE OF THE NEGATIVITY GERMS!
NYA HA HA HA...
BZZZZ...

HEARING ME TALK LIKE THIS MUST BE ANNOYING, HUH?!
I'M ANNOYING, RIGHT?! YOU THINK I'M ANNOYING DON'T YOU?!
UHHH... NO...?
GRAAAAAH! HOW CAN I BE A WORTHY BUTLER IF YOU CAN'T EVEN TELL ME YOUR TRUE FEELINGS?! TELL ME I'M ANNOYING!
NO, I DON'T THINK YOU ARE!
YOU'RE LYING TO ME! I KNOW YOU'RE ANNOYED! QUIT HOLDING BACK!
HUH?! HUH?! HUH?!
GAAAAH! FINE!
YOU'RE ANNOY-ING!
YOU'RE REALLY ANNOYING!

HE'S STILL FREAKING OUT!
SO ANNOYING...
MY MASTER'S ANNOYED BY ME!
IT'S ALL OVER NOW!
LOOK OUT, HAPPIERRE!
FWUNT
NOT SO FAST! NEGATIVITY GERMS!
!!
SMILE! ♪
HAPPI-ERRE, HELP ME!

THU
NG K
HAPPY !!
FSSSH...
NO! MY GERMS CAN'T STAND UP TO THE POWER OF HAPPI-NESS!
VNNN
HAPPY !!
YOU CAN DO IT!
FWUNT
I WON'T BE DEFEATED! HAVE ANOTHER HELPING OF NEGATIVITY GERMS!
HAPPY !!

WONK WONK
AW, WHAT'S THE POINT...
THIS ISN'T EXACTLY AN AMUSE-MENT PARK.
GAAAAH! HE LOST!
UNGH... I RELEASED TOO MANY... NEGATIVITY GERMS FROM MY BODY...
TWITCH TWITCH
I'M OUT OF... NEGATIVE POWER... NEED TO REPLENISH...
WHAT SHOULD WE DO, WHISPER...?
WHAT CAN WE DO? NOTHING! JUST FORGET IT...
PLORP
HEY...ARE YOU A NEGATIVE YO-KAI? I'M PRETTY NEGATIVE TOO.
I CAN TELL. BUT I'M MORE NEGATIVE THAN YOU ARE.
WONK WONK...
YOU CHAL-LENG-ING ME?
NOT THAT I'D EVER WIN...
WILL YOU STOP TRYING TO OUT-NEGATIVE EACH OTHER ?!
HEH ...

THOSE NEGATIVE FEELINGS ARE MINE!
THUNGK
AAARGH!
VOOSH
SLURP SLURP
GULP GULP
SLURP SLURP SLURP SLURP
HUH?
NNNGH...
WHAT ?!
NEGATIVITY GERMS GROW INSIDE PEOPLE WHO ARE NEGATIVE...
GULP GULP
AND THAT'S WHAT I FEED ON.
NEGATIVE POWER FULL CHARGE!
FWAASH
YEAH, I DON'T FEEL LIKE I'LL EVER DO ANYTHING RIGHT!
THIS IS THE END OF THE LINE!
THAT'S NOT EXACTLY SCARY...
THE STRONGER HE GETS, THE MORE NEGATIVE HE BECOMES.
!!
WHISPER, HOW ARE YOU --?

WHAAAAAT?!
IT'S AN HONOR TO BE YOUR BUTLER, NATE! ♪
WHAAAAA
WHAT HAPPENED ?!
BZZZZZ
WHEN I DEVOUR SOMEONE'S NEGATIVE GERMS, THEY BECOME POSITIVE AND OPTIMISTIC ...
WHAT ?!

THAT'S AWESOME! SO MANY PEOPLE COULD USE THAT! ♪
YOU SHOULD USE IT TO HELP PEOPLE!
NO WAY.
I HELPED THAT GUY BECAUSE HE'S A YO-KAI.
HUMANS CAN'T BE TRUSTED, THOUGH. WHO KNOWS WHEN THEY'LL START EXTERMINATING US?
I'LL TURN THEM ALL INTO NEGATIVE PEOPLE, THEN KEEP THEM ALIVE TO FEED ON!
...
NATE, WHY DON'T YOU JUST TRY BEING NEGATIVE? IT'S NOT THAT BAD, REALLY.
VOOOSH
YOU CAN'T BE POSITIVE ABOUT BEING NEGATIVE!
NOW I'LL START WITH YOU!
BZZZZZ...
I'VE GOT NO CHOICE... TIME TO SUMMON HIM...
VOOSH
KR RKT
YO-KAI MEDAL, DO YOUR THING!
CALLING...
VN NNNNN

RRRRRRR
JIBANYAN!!
RRRR

WHOEVER YOU SUMMON, I'LL TURN THEM NEGATIVE!
JIBANYAN, I NEED YOUR HELP!

I'M...
...DONE FOR...
HE'S ALREADY NEGATIVE ?!
WONK-WONK
WHAT'S WRONG?
I LOST A LOT OF MONEY.
OH... I'M SO SORRY, JIBA-NYAN...
I HOPE HE GETS OVER IT...
BUT WHY DID A YO-KAI HAVE MONEY ...?

I FOUND IT ON THE ROAD EARLIER!
WAUUUUUUGH
I REALLY WANTED TO BUY SOME FRESH JUICE!
YOU FOUND IT?! THEN WHY DO YOU CARE?!
HE COMES OUT EVEN IN THE END!
WHAM
WHAM
HERE! TAKE MY ALLOWANCE...
...NOW CHEER UP!
DON'T PLAY AROUND WITH ME!
CHA-CHING
I DON'T NEED YOUR MONEY TO GET TO WORK!
YOUR EYES!!
MEOW!
I DON'T KNOW WHY... BUT I FEEL SO MUCH BETTER!
ISN'T THAT OBVIOUS?!

FWUN—T
NEGATIVITY GERMS! DON'T INHALE THEM, JIBANYAN!!
I CAN'T... NO MORE ...!
HEY! THEY'RE WORKING TOGETHER!
WHISPER, WE NEED TO WORK TOGETHER TO HELP NATE!
I'D BE DELIGHTED! WHAT'S YOUR PLAN?
THIS WAY!

WHOOOOSH
YOU CAN DO IT, WHISPER!
NO! HE'S USING WHISPER TO SUCK UP ALL THE GERMS!
THEN I'LL JUST SEND OUT MORE GERMS!!
PFFFFT
OH NO, YOU WON'T! TAKE THIS...
PAWS OF...

FURY!!
CHOOM
CHOOM
CHOOM
CHOOM
CHOOM
CHOOM
CHOOM

NNNNGGH
CHOOM
HE DID IT!
BLU RB

URRKT!
PHOONT
HUUNH?!
AHHHH...
GLUB
GLUB
GLUB
MRAOW!
FWUMP
HEH...
I KNOW, I'M ALWAYS THE BUTT OF THE JOKE.
WELL... I'VE DONE MY PART NOW...
JIBANYAAAAN!!
URGH...
BZZZ...
SHUMP...
YOU STILL WON'T GIVE UP?!

I EXPELLED ALL MY NEGATIVITY GERMS AND I FEEL SO REFRESHED! ♪
LIFE IS SO BEAUTIFUL! ♪
OH ...

NOW DO YOU SEE HOW WONDERFUL YOUR POWER TO TAKE AWAY NEGATIVITY IS?!
YES...I'D NEVER THOUGHT OF IT BEFORE...
THANK YOU FOR MAKING ME UNDER-STAND.
WOULD YOU PLEASE BECOME MY FRIEND?
WHAT? OH, SURE.
PAP
VNNN-N-N...
HOORAY!
POPT
I GOT ANOTHER YO-KAI MEDAL! THE SIGN OF OUR FRIENDSHIP!

WE DID ALL THE WORK AND HE HASN'T EVEN THANKED US...
WONK WONK WONK
THE LITTLE GUYS LIKE US NEVER GET A FAIR SHAKE...
ARE THEY STILL GOING ...?!
I'M SORRY, BUT COULD YOU EAT THEIR NEGA-TIVE FEEL-INGS?
I-ING
OF COURSE! ♪
SLURP
SLURP
SLURP
SLURP
WE DIDN'T HELP YOU BECAUSE WE WANTED YOU TO THANK US... ♪
RIGHT?
RIGHT.
HAPPY!
RIGHT. ♪ WE HELPED YOU BECAUSE IT MAKES US HAPPY! ♪
YEAH. THIS IS MUCH BETTER. ♪
THANKS, NEGATI-BUZZ.

WHAA?!
THANKS? AW, YOU'RE JUST USING ME...
WONK WONK
TURNED BACK AFTER SLURPING UP THE NEGATIVE GERMS.
BUT I MADE A DEAL WITH YOU SO I GUESS I'LL HELP YOU FROM NOW ON...
EVEN THOUGH I DON'T WANT TO...
MUMBLE MUMBLE
YOU DON'T TRUST ME, DO YOU? HUH? HUH?
ANOTHER ANNOYING YO-KAI FRIEND... SIGH...
NATE ADAMS' CURRENT NUMBER OF YO-KAI FRIENDS: 8

POSITIVE THINKING
WONK-WONK
IT'S OVER
I THOUGHT YOU WERE BACK TO BEING POSITIVE!
SNIFF...
I RE-CEIVED 3 OUT OF 100 ON THE "BUTLER SKILLS TEST"...
AWW, DON'T WORRY...
I GET BAD GRADES SOME-TIMES TOO!
GRRRR R
BUT UNLIKE YOU, I TAKE MY TESTS SERI-OUSLY!
I DO TAKE MY TESTS SERI-OUSLY...
3 OUT OF 100? DID YOU EVEN STUDY?
WHAA AM
I THOUGHT I'D BE ABLE TO ACE IT WITH JUST A LITTLE LUCK!
WOW... THAT IS POSITIVE THINK-ING...

A BONUS CHAPTER STARTS ON THE NEXT PAGE!
THERE ARE ALSO FOUR BONUS FUNNIES IN THIS VOLUME.
WHAT?! BUT I ONLY SAW THREE BONUS FUNNIES!
TRY LOOKING FOR THE FOURTH ONE!

BONUS CHAPTER 1: LATE TO SCHOOL!!

HUNH?
WHAT?
MMM...
MY BUTLER?!
YOU'RE NOT EVEN AWAKE!
I FORGOT TO WAKE YOU! I'M A FAILURE AS A BUTLER!
THUD THUD
I'LL GIVE MY LIFE TO RE-PENT!
PLEASE DON'T! JUST GET ME TO SCHOOL ON TIME!
THUD THUD
...TO USE YOUR YO-KAI WATCH!
USE THE YO-KAI'S POWER TO GET TO SCHOOL ON TIME!
GO AHEAD! HURRY UP AND USE IT!
RR
UM
BB
MM
LB
LE
I CAN USE THE WATCH FOR SOME-THING LIKE THIS? REALLY?!
VERY WELL ...
NOW'S THE TIME...

FW-UMP
OF COURSE YOU CAN!
HAVE A NICE DAY AT SCHOOL.
GOOD NIGHT.
HE JUST WANTS TO STAY IN BED...!
VNN NN NN
CALLING ...
KRRRKT
DO YOUR THING!
HUMPH. YO-KAI MEDAL!
... JIBA-NYAN!
VNNN N N N
I'M LATE FOR SCHOOL! HELP ME GET THERE ON TIME!
HUNH?

...
WHA AM
YAAAWN
SORRY, I DIDN'T KNOW YOU WERE ASLEEP!!
THANKS, JIBAN-YAN!
MEOW
THIS ISN'T FAIR! I'LL BUY YOU A SODA IF YOU DO IT!
TAKING CARE OF ME IS ONLY WORTH A SODA?!
OH WELL... HOP ON MY BACK.
THANKS!
MEEEEEOOOOOOW!
TUMP
TUMP
TUMP
TUMP
TUMP
WOW! YOU'RE CRAZY FAST!
I'LL GET TO SCHOOL IN NO TIME!

KRA-THOOM
GRAAAAH
MRAAAAOW!!
BEEP BEEP
THEY WERE SO FAST THE DRIVER DIDN'T NOTICE THEM.
UNNNNGH...
I SHOULD HAVE JUST GONE IN LATE...
TWITCH TWITCH...

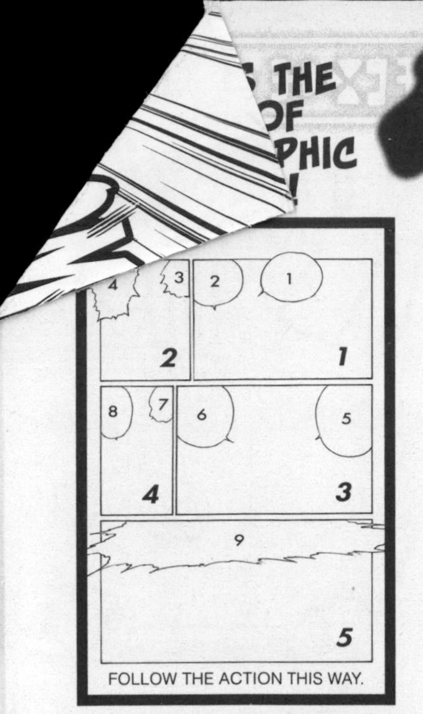

To properly enjoy this Perfect Square graphic novel, please turn it around and begin reading from right to left.

THE SECRET OF THE *YO-KAI WATCH*

AUTHOR BIO

This is where this manga was created.
—Noriyuki Konishi

Noriyuki Konishi hails from Shimabara City in Nagasaki Prefecture, Japan. He debuted with the one-shot *E-CUFF* in *Monthly Shonen Jump Original* in 1997. He is known for writing manga adaptations of *AM Driver* and *Mushiking: King of the Beetles*, along with *Saiyuki Hiro Go-Kū Den!*, *Chōhenshin Gag Gaiden!! Card Warrior Kamen Riders*, *Go-Go-Go Saiyuki: Shin Gokūden* and more.